To Jenny Rose, my wife, for making me write down my stories.
To Krista Rose Latiolais, my daughter, for teaching me how to be a dad.
To Holly Rose Lopez, my daughter, for always making me laugh.
To Joel Compton, my son, for always making me think.
To Madison Rose, my daughter, who in her short 25 years taught me to always "go for it" and to "live life to the fullest."
To Elena Ricevuto, for all her hard work checking our spelling and grammar.
To MaryJo Moore, for a wonderful web design, graphics, and dedication.
To Rayanne Vieira, for illustrating our visions.

To Javier Lopez, my son-in-law, for being an insightful poet and steady partner in this series of books.
— Don Rose

I dedicate this book to my awesome wife for always being there for me and loving me even when I'm annoying. You're the best! Also, to my four wild and crazy kiddos who keep me on my toes and help me want to escape to *When the Day Ends and Dreams Begin.* I also dedicate this book to all my nieces and nephews, whom I love very much. As a matter of fact, some of the poems and stories might be about you guys.
— Javier Lopez

www.mascotbooks.com
roselopezbooks.com

When the Day Ends... and Dreams Begin... 2

For more information, please contact:
Mascot Books
620 Herndon Parkway #320
Herndon, VA 20170
info@mascotbooks.com

Library of Congress Control Number: 2019910388

CPSIA Code: PRT0919A
ISBN-13: 978-1-64307-501-3

Printed in the United States

When the Day Ends... and Dreams Begin... 2

Don Rose & Javier Lopez

illustrated by Rayanne Vieira

Contents

Rocky the Rock, the Rock That Could Talk

Once there was a rock, not just any rock, but a special rock: Rocky the Rock. Rocky started out in the ocean, but he was determined to be on the warm beach with all the people having fun. With a little luck, and a brand new pair of legs, Rocky made it to the Carmel-by-the-Sea Beach to live and learn about people, birds, dogs, and all that the beach had to offer. Rocky was just so curious about life.

Rocky was careful not to get too close to the kids. Last time he was on the beach, someone had thrown him back into the cold ocean. But that was how he had gotten his legs in the first place. He was so angry, he rumbled and tumbled, steamed and stumbled, until suddenly two skinny legs popped out of him. When he made it to the shore, he tried to greet the other rocks, but no one answered because rocks don't talk!

But on this fine day, Rocky greeted a passing seagull with a pleasant "Hello." But the seagull just looked away.

Then "Hi," he said to a passing dog, but the dog just ran away. "Well," said Rocky, "I need to move down the beach to see if someone will talk to me." He moved slowly but surely down the beach, being careful not to be seen moving.

Soon, he approached a boy and girl tanning on the beach. "Hello," said Rocky.

"What?" asked the boy, thinking that the girl was talking to him.

"I didn't say anything," said the girl.

Rocky beamed; he was happy someone had heard him, but he was also happy that he had tricked them. *Haha*, thought Rocky. *This could be fun.*

"Where are we?" said Rocky.

The boy answered, "You know we are on Carmel-By-the–Sea Beach."

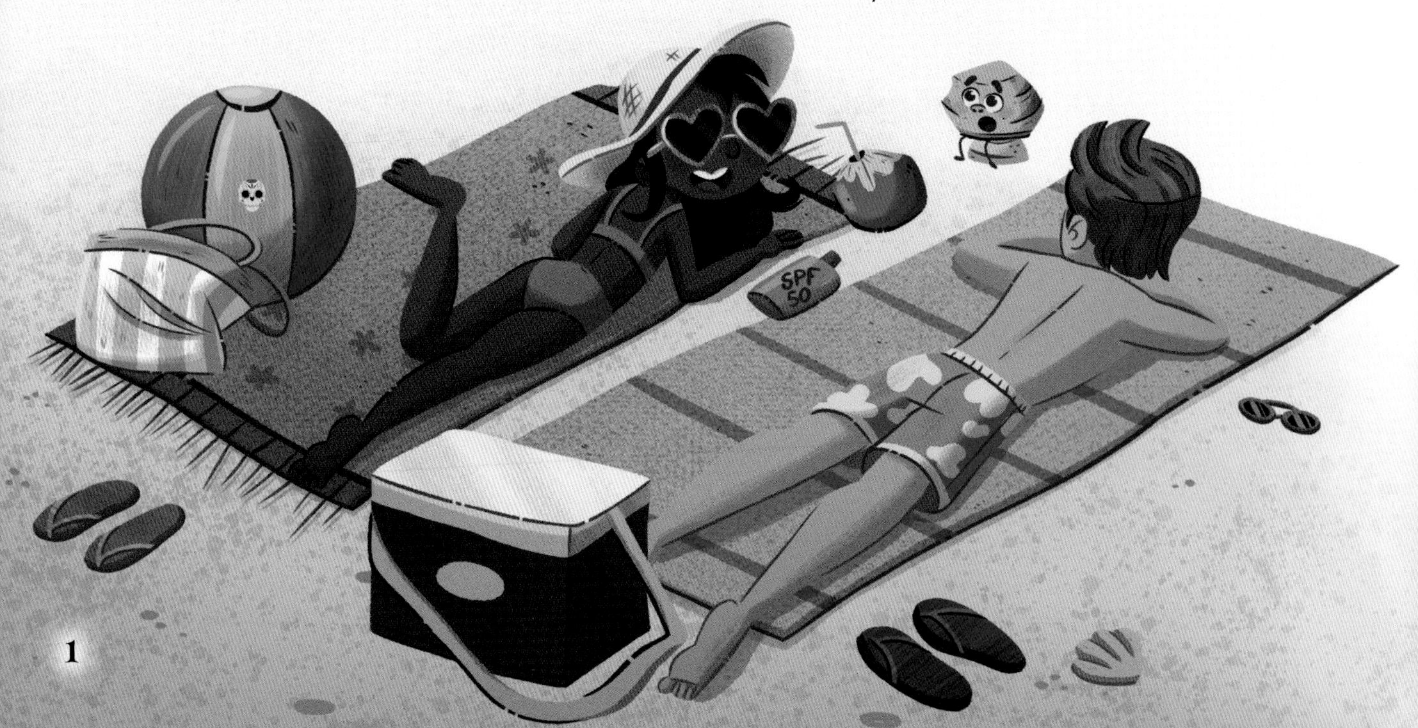

The girl just grunted at the boy, not understanding why he was telling her where they were.

"You sure are cute," Rocky whispered to the girl.

"Awwww," said the girl, and she reached for the boy's hand.

"What are you doing?!" asked the boy, surprised.

Rocky was about to say something else when a cute, fluffy, reddish-brown dog named Uncle Frank wandered by. "Hey! I heard what you said and that's not nice," said Uncle Frank.

"You can hear me?" said Rocky. "Only the people seem to hear me."

"Oh yeah, I can hear you," said Uncle Frank. "I'm out walking my mom and dad on the beach. They think they're walking me, but in reality, I'm walking them. It's good for them. They need the exercise, so I walk them around Casanova Street then to the 12th Avenue Beach every day."

"Wow," said Rocky. "That's so cool. I hope I see you later."

"Yes," replied Uncle Frank. "I've got to go walk my people. See you soon."

The next day, Rocky quietly walked up to a group of young adults on the beach. He sat amongst them, listening and waiting to say just the right thing.

One of the young men went to the ice chest and asked, "Does anyone want a soft drink?"

"Yeah, two," said Rocky. The young man looked around and didn't see anyone, so he put two soft drinks near Rocky and shrugged. "At least they weren't on my head this time!" Rocky laughed.

Next, the young man asked, "Anyone want a hot dog?"

"Yeah, I'll have one," answered Rocky. Once again, the young man put a hot dog down next to Rocky.

Just then, Uncle Frank wandered by. He saw the hot dog and ate it. "Thanks," Uncle Frank told Rocky gratefully.

"No problem," Rocky replied. "I think this could be the start of a great friendship."

Uncle Frank agreed with his mouth full.

So if you ever go to the Carmel-By-The-Sea Beach off 12th Avenue, be on the lookout for Rocky the Rock, the Rock That Could Talk, and his buddy, Uncle Frank.

The Answer

Once there was a boy named Andre who wondered what he might be when he grew up.

His dad was an accountant. He asked Andre, "Do you like working with numbers?" But he did not.

His mom was an interior designer. She asked, "Andre, would you like designing interior spaces for homes and offices?" But he did not.

He often spent time with his grandma and helped her in the kitchen, and he asked her what he might be.

His kind and gentle grandma said, "Andre, you'll be what you are meant to be. Now, hand me that towel and let's finish up this fresh pasta."

As they worked in the kitchen together, Andre started working on an apple strudel that he had learned how to make years ago while watching his grandma's masterful hands and listening to her simple instructions.

"Well, it might be fun to be a landscape architect, an architect, or an engineer, but I'm just not sure," he said.

"You still have plenty of time to decide. Just do something you love and have a passion for. Now, let's get started on the cheese bread for the meal," said Grandma.

As Andre worked quickly and expertly in the kitchen, he wondered about other jobs like being a plumber, an electrician, and maybe even a firefighter at a fire station. During another day in the kitchen with Grandma, he began talking about different types of jobs.

"Pass the steaks and start the marinade, if you would, please," said Grandma. Andre quickly put together garlic, salt and pepper, oil, vinegar, soy sauce, lemon, and white wine. He quickly whisked them together and handed the sauce to Grandma to float the steaks in. Next, he prepared savory Swiss sausage that they would grill for dinner tonight.

As Andre put the fresh bread in the oven, he said, "Grandma, the thing that makes me the happiest is working with you to get meals ready. It's fun, challenging, and there are so many different types of cooking techniques so I never get bored."

"Andre, I told you to find something you are passionate about and love to do. All these years in the kitchen together have been the happiest for me. I think you've discovered what you need to be: a chef!" said Grandma with a twinkle in her eye.

"Wow," said Andre. "All this time the answer's been right in front of me. Thank you, Grandma!" said Andre.

"You're welcome, Chef Andre!"

"This is the best day of my life!" smiled Andre.

The Pirate and the Mermaid

There once was a pirate as grumpy as could be,
But happiness he'd find when he'd sail the sea.
He loved the smell of the ocean and the breeze on his face.
The saltiness in the air, oh, how he loved the taste.
But something was brewing amongst his crew.
A mutiny they were planning because of what he wouldn't do.
They wanted to attack other ships and take all their loot
And load up their cannons and start to shoot.
They loved to plunder and look for other ships to scare.
For all of that madness the captain did not care.
He just wanted to sail and take in the view,
So of all this mutiny he had no clue.
With a blink of an eye, it happened so quick,
They all rushed the captain and he lost his ship.
He was in shock and couldn't believe
That his crew had done this and wanted him to leave.
When you're on a ship on the sea, there's only one place to go.
They made him walk the plank and yelled, "Look out below!"
He could hear them laughing as they sailed away.
He couldn't believe that this happened today.
Hours had passed as he floated in the sea.
But then, he felt something against his knee.
It's a shark, he thought. *I'm going to be its dinner.*
Oh, how I wish I was an excellent swimmer.
He tried not to be nervous but felt fear deep in his bones
And thought to himself, *I'm going to meet Davy Jones!*
But boy, was he wrong, and got a big surprise,
For a mermaid stood right before his eyes.
"Are you a siren," he asked, "who's going to make me drown?"
The mermaid looked bewildered and began to frown.
"No," she said. "Why would I do such a thing?"

He told her, "I heard stories from songs pirates would sing."
"I'm here to help you and take you to land."
"No thank you, miss, I don't need a hand."
"But you will surely drown if I leave you alone."
"It's okay, miss, I no longer have a home.
The crew took my ship, I have nothing left."
Silly man, she thought. *Just take another breath.*
So she grabbed him by his collar and began to swim.
She found him an island; she really saved him.
"Sir, I know you are sad, but life must go on.
Gather up your feelings. It's time to be strong.
Something bad has happened, but life does not stop.
In a bad situation, you find yourself caught.
But lace up your boots and roll those sleeves up.
Life is what you make of it—pour some rum in your cup."
He asked her, "Why did you help me and bring me to this place?"
"I was swimming next to your ship and saw the smile on your face.
I thought, 'There is a person who's happy and so full of might.
Letting someone like that drown, well, that wouldn't be right!'
But to be honest with you, I don't like how that sounds.
Truth be told, I would not let anyone drown."
The captain was smitten with her and how sweet she was.
He couldn't believe it, but he was in love.
"I don't know your name, miss, what could it be?"
"It's a pleasure to meet you, sir, my name is Holly."
The pirate made a vow to her to make the most of his life
Under one condition: if she would become his wife.
"But we just met, sir, and your name I don't know."
"It's Xavier, my love, and you have captured my soul."
"But I am a mermaid and you are a man."
"No worries, my dear, I do have a plan."
I will stop the story here till next time, my friend,
But be well aware that this isn't the end.

Different

We may not look the same, but different we are not.
There's no need for name calling,
So will you please stop?
My skin may be dark or it may be light.
You may have perfect vision or need glasses for sight.
Some have legs to run, while others need chairs to move.
Let me be me, as I let you be you.
We all may look different, but inside we are the same.
One stomach, two lungs, one heart, and one brain.
Let's stop the bullying and treat others kind.
You never know, in that person a best friend you might find.
So next time you see someone different who is not the same,
Invite them over to join your game.

Camping

One day, when it was raining and cold outside, my dad started talking about taking me camping next year during the warm summer.

"What's camping?" I asked.

"Well," said Dad, "it's living outdoors in nature, a wonderful experience I think you're ready for. Here, we live in a house, made of wood and stone, but when we go camping, we'll live in a tent made out of nylon that we put up in a campsite. It's like a small house that you and I will sleep in.

"Here, we sleep in beds, but when we go camping, we'll sleep in a soft sleeping bag to stay warm at night. To make our beds even more comfortable, we'll sleep on an air mattress that'll keep us off the ground and make sure we get a good night's sleep.

"At home, we cook our breakfast in the kitchen over a family stove. When we go camping, we'll cook outside over a small camp stove. At night, we'll use the camp stove and a campfire that we'll build. The campfire will keep us warm until we go to bed. But before we go to bed, we'll cook s'mores over the campfire. To make s'mores, you roast marshmallows and then put them between two graham crackers and rich chocolate. Yummy! They're called s'mores because when you finish one you want 'some more.'

"When we go camping, during the day we can take hikes and explore, go swimming in the lake, ride horses, play in the creek, and even sit in a chair in the shade and read a good book.

"At night, we can sit around the campfire and talk, tell stories, talk about you growing up so fast, talk about what the future may hold, and—my favorite—tell jokes.

"One of the best things about camping is looking up at the thousands of stars at night. It's like being at home, but better, because at night in the mountains the stars shine so brightly they look like diamonds sparkling. Often you can see falling or shooting stars.

"Camping lets you get closer to nature where the air seems fresher, the night sounds are clearer, and the trees, shrubs, and flowers are bright and spectacular."

"Wow, camping sounds great! I can't wait for the summer to get here, Dad."

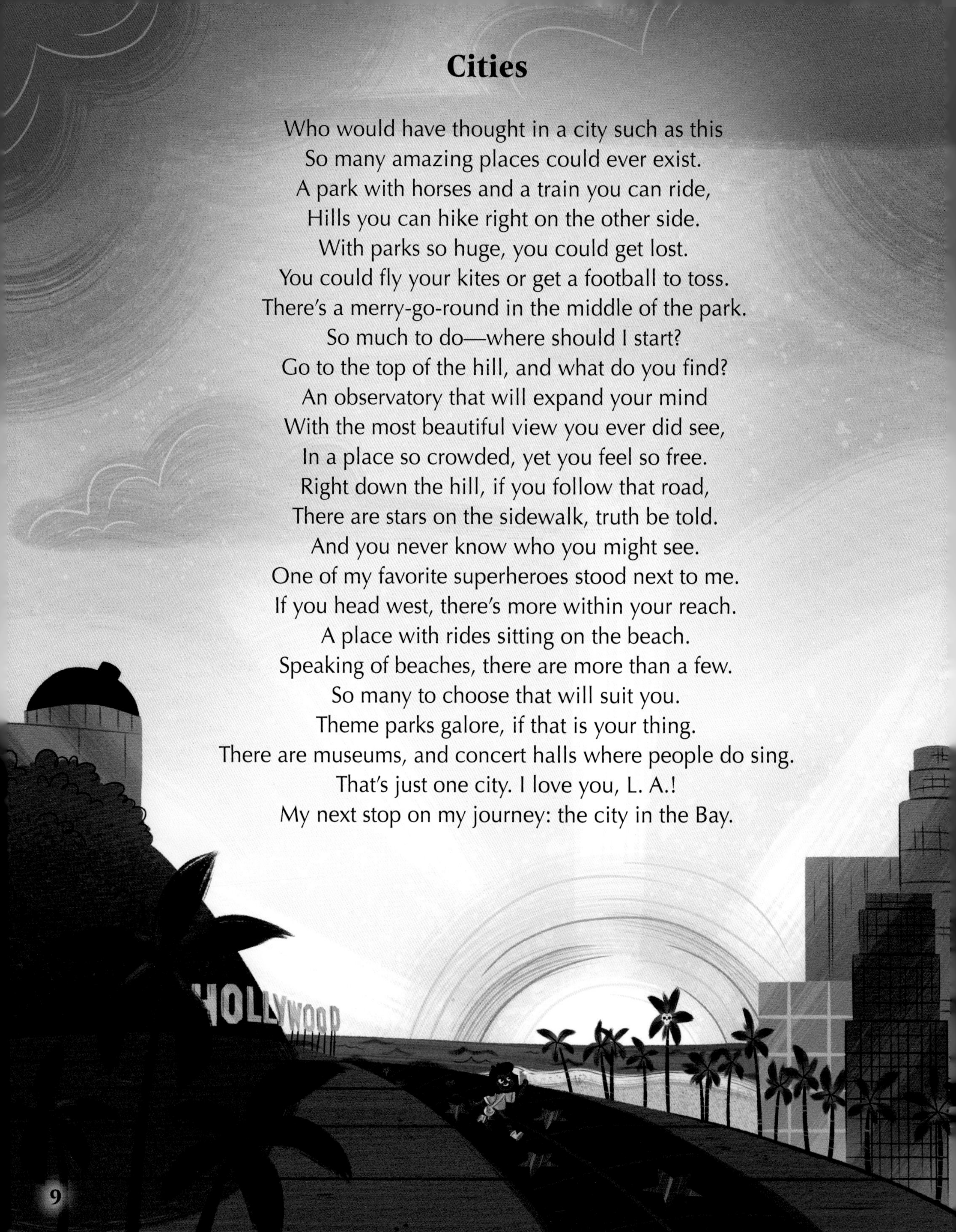

Cities

Who would have thought in a city such as this
So many amazing places could ever exist.
A park with horses and a train you can ride,
Hills you can hike right on the other side.
With parks so huge, you could get lost.
You could fly your kites or get a football to toss.
There's a merry-go-round in the middle of the park.
So much to do—where should I start?
Go to the top of the hill, and what do you find?
An observatory that will expand your mind
With the most beautiful view you ever did see,
In a place so crowded, yet you feel so free.
Right down the hill, if you follow that road,
There are stars on the sidewalk, truth be told.
And you never know who you might see.
One of my favorite superheroes stood next to me.
If you head west, there's more within your reach.
A place with rides sitting on the beach.
Speaking of beaches, there are more than a few.
So many to choose that will suit you.
Theme parks galore, if that is your thing.
There are museums, and concert halls where people do sing.
That's just one city. I love you, L. A.!
My next stop on my journey: the city in the Bay.

Anxiety

Do you ever never get nervous while your legs wobble in place?
Your heart starts racing and redness covers your face.
You don't know what just happened, but so nervous you've become.
Your fingertips start to tingle and sometimes you feel numb.
You feel as if you and other kids aren't the same.
And now your stomach's upset with all these thoughts in your brain.
Just go ahead and relax, and know you are not alone.
There are others who go through this, even some who are grown.
It's called anxiety and it's like a battle in your mind.
Take a deep breath and know you are fine.
I know you are thinking, *Fine I am not.*
In an endless cycle, I find myself caught.
It happens so often and I can't escape.
This nervous feeling, I really do hate.
Just take a deep breath and let it out slow.
Think happy thoughts and let the nervousness go.
It will take some practice, more than one try.
But don't ever give up; let me tell you why.
You're stronger than you think, trust me, I know.
Be brave and fight with your heart, mind, and soul.
When this happens to me, do you know what I do?
I play music I love to help get me through.
If I have no access to music, and I feel like I'm done,
I'll think of a memory where I had so much fun.
There are moments when crowds are just too much.
I don't want to talk or feel the slightest touch.
That's okay if you need a moment for yourself.
But remember, isolation is bad for your health.
So find that one thing that puts a smile on your face
To help calm you down and rescue you from that place.
Never let yourself think that you're all alone.
What you feel inside, let it be known.
Because when you speak up, you might just see
There are others who feel like you and me.

What I Want to be When I Grow Up

I'm pretty sure that when I grow up, I want to be a fireman. I'll rescue people in need, I'll put out fires, I'll get kittens out of trees, and I'll be able to slide down the fire pole in the fire station to get to the truck quickly. I'll get to drive the big, red fire truck and go fast down the streets with my siren blaring.

Yes. Being a fireman is for me.

Or…

I'll join the military and protect my country. I'll be a part of a big team and learn to parachute out of a plane in the Air Force. Maybe I'll be a pilot of a jet or be an Army Ranger. How about a Navy Seal? I'll travel the world and see so many things.

Yes, the military is for me.

Or…

Maybe I'll be a nurse, where I can help people who are sick, help with children, and care for people. Maybe I'll be a doctor who operates on people to save their lives, or maybe I'll be a veterinarian, who is a doctor for cats, dogs, and other animals.

Yes. The medical field is for me.

Or…

How about a landscape architect who designs all things outside: parks, lakes, schools, pools and golf courses? I would know all the plants and trees and flowers so I could design gardens. Or maybe I'll be an architect who creates houses and stores. Or maybe I'll be a contractor who builds the structures and parks.

Yes. The construction field is for me.

Or…

Maybe I'll be a teacher who works in schools and helps young students understand all the things in life. I'll teach sciences like biology and nutrition. Or I could teach sports like volleyball and basketball. Or I could teach different types of art, like drawing and ceramics. I think it would be fun to teach young people my age. I like my teachers.

Yes. A teacher's life is for me.

Or…

There are many choices that are interesting and fun. I'll have to decide when I get bigger, but there sure are a lot of great professions.

The Climbing Tree

Once upon a time, a long time ago, there was a magnificent oak tree living in a great meadow on the outskirts of town. This big oak produced lots of acorns each year that fed the birds, squirrels, and all the surrounding animals. There was one particular acorn that lived at the top of the old oak tree. He said, “Someday, I want to be a large oak like my parent.”

One windy, rainy day when there was a big storm, the little acorn was ready and detached himself from the big oak. He flew through the air as far as he could go. He continued to rumble and tumble, and turned over and over until he landed in a little crack in the earth that was wet and moist. It was a great place for a little oak to begin growing.

There he began to get rooted in the soil and started to grow. Like a juvenile, he was initially gangly and awkward, but he was developing good roots and a strong trunk. As the years went by, the little oak was growing bigger and stronger with the help of lots of rain and sun. It was a great place for an oak to grow.

As the town grew bigger, developers began to build houses in the area. Because of the oaks, they decided to call this development “Oak Meadows.” Oak Meadows was a great place for people to live. Developers sectioned off the land into lots and began building homes.

The little oak was in the backyard of a beautiful house that was being built. When the house was ready, a family moved in with their little children. They didn't know the oak tree yet. They saw it, but they weren't quite sure about it.

As the children started to get older, the oldest of the three wanted to start climbing the oak. The oak thought this was a great idea and wanted the child to climb him. He started to put branches out low to the ground.

As the children grew, they were able to get on the oak and climb a little bit. The oak said, "This is great; I love being a climbing tree." So he began to put branches out to the right and to the left and he let the kids climb him. It was so much fun for the children and the oak tree as they all grew.

One day, they moved away. The children had grown up, went off to college, and the family moved out of the house. They were gone.

The little oak was happy that he had been so much a part of their life, but he was also a little sad because they were gone.

The house was sold and a new family moved in with children. "This is great! I get to be a climbing tree again," he said. As he continued to grow, he kept some branches close to the ground. In the distance, he saw the big, magnificent oak and thought, *Someday, I'd like to be a great oak like my parent.*

The new family moved in, and they had two boys who loved to climb the tree up and down and around. There was also a little girl who lived in the house, and she didn't really want to climb, but she wanted to swing from the tree. The oak put out a special branch that could hold a rope swing. The dad put two ropes over the branch and attached a swing to them. The little girl swung back and forth as her brothers climbed the oak.

It was so fun for the oak. There was a new family to enjoy, and the family enjoyed the oak. The old, majestic tree could see the young oak in the distance, and it was happy.

The oak began to make shade in the backyard, and now even the parents began to enjoy the oak by having picnics under the tree. Everyone was happy.

The day came when once again the kids grew up and were off to college, and the parents put the house up for sale.

Another family moved in, and again the oak was delighted. Now the oak was a big selling point to the property because it was getting to be a pretty good size, and people began wanting to live in this house simply because of the big oak in the backyard. The new family loved to have picnics under the oak where it was cool and shady while the kids climbed and laughed. The swing was used by the children and the adults. The oak was so happy he had plenty of sun and moisture to grow bigger and stronger. This was the third family, and the oak was so pleased to be a part of them all.

The oak provided shade and a swing, but his proudest accomplishment was being a climbing tree. He loved when occasionally the families would drive by the property and say, "There is my oak tree. It's the tree I used to climb, the tree I used to swing on." And the big oak would smile.

How to be a Ninja

What I'm about to share are secrets I've learned.
They were taught to me, so now it's my turn.
I pass on this knowledge, extending my hand,
So you can become a ninja and join my clan.
First and foremost, before you read on,
You have to ask yourself if you're mentally strong.
You cannot be weak-minded or willing to quit.
So I hope you are ready—here we go, this is it!
You must keep it to yourself and not tell a soul,
Remaining hidden at all times is truly the goal.
You can practice on your siblings to perfect some tricks,
Set up traps for them and places to slip.
And try disappearing when your parents find out
Because they'll come looking and you'll hear them shout.
Work on your flips and running really fast,
Conquering all things, no matter the task.
Master your weapons, because in them you will trust.
Those paper towel nunchuks are awesome—definitely a must.
Make ninja stars to learn how to throw
And before you know it, you'll be a pro.
Be respectful of nature, you two will become one.
It will help keep you hidden under the bright sun.
There's so much to learn, but let's pause right here.
These things you must master and this stage you must clear.
I will be watching to see if you remain steady,
And more lessons I'll teach when I know that you're ready.

The Big Red Shiny Balloon

Once there was a big red shiny balloon that just couldn't wait for someone to stop by and bring her home.

Soon a mom came by and selected the red balloon to be a part of her daughter's tenth birthday party. *Oh boy, oh boy*, thought the big red shiny balloon. *I get to be part of a big celebration*.

The big red shiny balloon bounced all over the car on the way home. The red balloon was so excited that she almost got out of the car too soon, but the mom grabbed her by her pretty white ribbon.

Soon a birthday girl came running down the stairs and happily took the balloon for a run around the house.

"Here's my room," said the pretty brown-haired girl. "And here's my kitchen with my birthday cake, and here is the backyard with all my friends and family."

"What a beautiful big red shiny balloon," everyone said. The balloon was beaming.

There were decorations, good food, and lots of talking and laughing going on. *How exciting*, thought the balloon.

Soon everyone was done eating and the birthday cake was brought out with ten glowing candles. The birthday girl laughed and sang her birthday song with everyone else.

Never letting go of the big red shiny balloon, the birthday girl ate her cake and opened her presents. Finally, the birthday was coming to an end. All the kids said, "Let's let the big red shiny balloon go and we'll watch it for as long as we can."

Yes, thought the balloon.

"Yes," said the birthday girl.

There was great anticipation and an enthusiastic countdown: "3, 2, 1... GO!"

The little girl gently let the big red shiny balloon go into the clear and beautiful blue sky.

First slowly, and then with a bit more speed, the balloon rose. *Yahoooo*, thought the balloon as the children got smaller and smaller and the world got bigger and bigger.

The children laughed and waved at the balloon, and the balloon waved her pretty white ribbon back and forth.

The big shiny red balloon soon floated out of sight of the kids; she was having the time of her life.

"Wheeee, this is so fun! I am up so far and I can see so much."

The big red shiny balloon, with her pretty white ribbon, was seeing the world.

If you ever look up and see a big red shiny balloon, wave and say "Hi!" as she passes on her way to more adventures.

Dads

Dads are awesome if you ask me.
They teach you things like climbing a tree
And all about fishing, putting the worm on a hook.
Or being in the kitchen, teaching you how to cook.
Some go to work in the morning and work all through the day,
But as soon as they get home, they find time to play.
Mine has tea parties with my sister or with me has a race.
My sister loves to put makeup all over our dad's face.
He doesn't even mind it—he thinks he looks great.
He looks in the mirror and funny faces he makes.
One day while driving he came to a stop
To help an old lady with the groceries she dropped.
He's like a superhero, trying to help all,
And you should see how far he can throw a football.
There are so many types of dads out there you can see.
Right next to my dad is where you'll find me.

Siblings

I have three siblings and we're not the same.
That we share the same blood sometimes boggles my brain.
We are quite different, yes, this is true.
Sometimes my mind's blown by the things that they do.
I am younger than the other three.
Two brothers, one sister, and then there is me.
My oldest brother sometimes I can't even grasp,
The actions he takes and the questions he asks.
But when I need to be silly, he'll play right along.
He loves to rhyme words, and he wrote his own song.
My second oldest brother is as wild as can be,
But he doesn't hesitate to take silly pictures with me.
He's gotten in trouble from choices he's made,
And quite a few consequences my brother has paid.
Sometimes he has a temper, but our dad tells him "stop."
Because on my dad's bad side he doesn't want to get caught.
Then there's my sister, as tough as can be.
She even gets tough when it comes to me.
You should see her eyes roll and the looks she can make.
It's like she stares right through your soul, for goodness' sake.
But she has my back no matter what.
If someone messes with me, you best believe she'll show up
To stand by my side and protect her lil' sis.
Bullies beware! She hits with closed fists.
Sometimes they drive me crazy and I just want to scream.
Rattling my nerves and being so mean,
They can make me so mad, my anger flies off the chart.
But no matter what, I love them with all of my heart.

I Am Me

Am I the tallest, strongest, most handsome boy in the world? Am I the smartest, richest, most athletic boy ever?

No, I am not.

I am none of those things and I really don't want to be any of those things. I am of average height and I am an average athlete. I am not unusually strong or handsome.

What I do is try my best every day. I am smart, but only because I pay attention in school to my teachers. I read books every day and I discuss everything with my parents and friends.

I am me and I am proud of that fact.

If I feel my weight is more than I want it to be, I walk more and eat less. If I feel I need to gain weight, I walk more and eat more.

To be strong, I walk, go to the gym, and eat healthy. Although I do like sweets, I ration them, but I do not deny them.

I am me and I like me.

I try to smile more, be positive, help my friends, and be kind. People like me because I like them and I like me.

My opinions are honest and from the heart. I will listen to your opinion and we can discuss the differences.

I want to live a good life, so I work hard at whatever I do. I also love to laugh and I find many things in life are funny—especially my best friend, my dog Uncle Frank.

To think positive is important, but I know that there are bad things in life, too. I need to know what they are so I can combat them whenever I can.

I want to learn a profession that I will love, put all my energy into, and make a good living from. I am willing to put in the time and effort into learning a profession from those who have lots of experience.

I want to spend time giving back to my community, to help where I can when I can.

To help others, I must like me, trust me, and be the best me that I can be.

You must do this, too. It is a path you must embrace, and once you have confidence, you will see you are you, and that is a good thing.

Two Sides to a Story 2

Shoo fly, leave me alone.
How did you ever get into my home?
Being so bothersome, flying all around,
Driving me crazy with that buzzing sound.
All around my face, down to my feet,
Even bothering me when I'm about to eat.
So I'll grab my fly swatter and swat you out of the sky,
Make you go squish so you can no longer fly.
You should have thought twice before bothering me.
Once I get you, then you will see.

Wow, I'm no longer crawling on the ground.
I got a new body with wings that make a cool sound.
I can fly here and there, wherever I please.
Up so high, I soar past the trees.
This is amazing; my life is so great.
There's so much to explore, I cannot wait.
I'm gonna follow that person walking inside his home.
I'll show him my new wings and how I have grown.
I'll fly towards his face so we could talk.
Better yet, I'll wait till he no longer walks.
What's that he has? It smells so good.
I hope he shares, you know he should.
When I got close to him, he waved his hand.
He invited me over just like I planned.
All of a sudden, he wants to play,
Swinging this thing every which way.
He seems so nice, I hope he can be my friend.
This game is so fun! I hope it never ends.

The Little Girl with a Bag Over Her Head

When Maddie was a little girl, she loved her mom and dad. She lived in a house with her two older sisters, Krista and Holly, and her brother, Joel. She loved her house with all the noise and activity.

When Mom said, "Okay, it's time to clean your room," everybody went to clean their rooms. Not very well, mind you, but off they went.

Mom would say things that Maddie did not fully understand. She would say, "I love you to the moon and back," or "You make–a-me-crazy," or "A penny for your thoughts?"

But some things she did understand, such as, "Someone please take the garbage out; it's beginning to smell!"

One day when mom was very busy and a little grumpy and distracted, she said something to Maddie that was startling. "If one more kid leaves the kitchen in a big mess and does not clean up after themselves, I'm going to break every bone in their body."

Uh-oh, thought Maddie, *I'm not sure what that means, but it's not going to be me who gets every bone in my body broken.* She quickly went to her room, got a big brown paper grocery bag, and cut out two big holes for her eyes.

She walked into the living room. Mom was now relaxed and happy. She looked up and saw Maddie with a big bag over her head. "Now, who is that?" asked Mom with a smile.

Maddie said, "No one."

Mom laughed. "Now, what's going on?"

"I don't want every bone in my body broken," Maddie said.

"What?" asked Mom. "Who said that?"

"You did," said Maddie.

Mom laughed, gently took the bag off Maddie's head, and said, "That was wrong of me to say; I will never say that again."

Mom laughed and hugged Maddie. As she did this, the other three kids walked into the living room. All three children had big brown paper grocery bags over their heads with the eyes cut out.

"Oh my," said Mom. "I'll have to be more careful about what I say."

And they all laughed and took the bags off their heads—all except Holly. "I'm not taking my bag off just yet," she said.

And they all laughed harder.

Mighty Girl

"You throw like a girl." What does that mean?
That I throw like a champ with the elegance of a queen?
I can't join your club called "No Girls Allowed."
Don't be weak minded; break away from the crowd.
Who made that rule anyway, a boy who is weak?
When he's around a girl, somehow he can't speak.
I didn't want to join anyway; I didn't think twice.
It smells really bad and it doesn't look very nice.
I just like to play sports of every kind
And a willing opponent I have yet to find.
So let me join the game and give me no grief.
And if you say girls can't play, then I'll knock out your teeth!

Hey Spider

Hey there Spider, would you please let me be?
I notice all your eyes just staring at me.
You rub your legs together as if you're looking at a treat.
Don't you know I'm a lot bigger and I have two huge feet?
I don't want to stomp you and make your body go squish,
But if you don't leave me alone, I'll do as you wish.
Hey there, Spider, don't get any closer.
I see you climbing up my wall trying to blend into my poster.
You're not as sneaky as you assume.
If you go any higher, I will hit you with a broom.
I'm watching you, Spider. Where do you intend to go?
Right to your web? Well, wouldn't you know.
What's that in your web, twitching all around?
It's that annoying mosquito with its buzzing sound.
You eat mosquitoes? Well, that's a great sight to see.
It looks like good friends the both of us shall be.
I don't like those skeeters and how they bite.
Hey Spider, if you keep eating them, we'll be all right.

Teachers

Did you know teachers are superheroes, and battles they fight?
You're probably thinking, *Whatever, uh-huh, yeah right.*
Seriously, I witnessed it with my own two eyes.
Oh, the horrors they faced! I can still hear the cries.
The monsters are wild, they can't be tamed.
I don't know how teachers do it; I'd go insane.
You have clowns that are crazy, who bring a different type of wrath,
Who do what they can just to get others to laugh.
Then there's the wild ones, who give off nothing but sass.
They don't even think twice about disrupting the class.
How about chatter monsters whose talking won't quit?
And some with ants in their pants who don't know how to sit.
You think there's no monsters for you to see,
But to be honest with you, one of those monsters was me.
When I grew up, I apologized for what the monster in me did.
The teacher said, "I didn't see a monster, I just saw a kid."
At that very moment, I realized what teachers do.
No matter the chaos around them, they'll still teach you.
When the last bell rings around three o' clock,
The work for the teachers doesn't really stop.
They get home, grade papers, and plan for the next day.
While we get to go home, relax, have fun, and just play.
They go above and beyond to teach us right from wrong,
Helping build our confidence and making our minds strong.
There are special teachers if you pay attention and look,
Who not only teach you by reading a book.
There are school counselors who teach us how to cope.
When we're worried and overwhelmed, they help fill us with hope.
To all of those teachers that put up with me,
When I look at you, a superhero I see.

Nicolas

Once there was a French boy named Nicolas who just loved swimming in his new family swimming pool. It was a big, rectangular pool with steps that led into the deep, blue-gray water. Nicholas knew how to swim, and his mother, Sophie, bought him a facemask and fins to swim and explore the new pool with its clear, cool water.

The family was so pleased to have a way to cool off during the long, warm summer days in Bordeaux, France, with their new beautiful pool. When they went into the pool, they laughed, splashed, and enjoyed the water.

But when Nicolas went into the pool with his facemask and fins, he was an explorer and could see the wonderful things the pool brought.

He swam with his face under the water, breathing through the snorkel. He saw two beautiful green sea turtles swim slowly by. He saw a coral reef on the bottom with beautiful green, orange, yellow, red, and blue fish—some fish with many colors, and some with solid colors. They swam lazily by as Nicolas observed them. In the distance, a family of dolphins swam together, often leaping into the air, then diving deep into the water.

The pool was alive with all types of sea creatures.

When Nicolas told his mother about the wonderful world he experienced in the pool, she just laughed and said she did not see turtles or dolphins, but just cool, pure water.

Nicolas was confused, but thrilled his backyard held such a wonderful, wonderful world within the pool's waters.

Every day, as soon as he was finished with breakfast and cleaning his room, he headed out to his wonderland pool to explore what the day would bring.

A very big, very long, and very wide whale swam slowly by with a baby whale that, while not as big as his mom, was still very large to Nicolas.

When he got out of the pool for the day, Nicolas researched all the wonderful things he saw in the pool. He learned all about coral reefs, dolphins, sea turtles, whales, and the many colorful fish.

Nicolas began to love the oceans, seas, and large bodies of water that dominate our planet Earth.

As Nicolas grew older, he began to study this environment. He studied oceanography and marine biology, and soon became an expert on the oceans and how to maintain, preserve, and protect our wonderful waters with their abundance of life.

Nicolas never forgot his pool and would often visit his parents and go for a swim in his personal wonderland pool. It was a very magical pool indeed.

The Bike Ride

When I was a boy, I would wake up early on Saturdays, eat breakfast, and then hurry up and do my chores: mowing the front and back lawns with a push mower, taking the garbage out of the house to the garbage pails on the side of the house, and taking all the used newspapers and tying them into bundles in the garage.

And then…

Freedom! My parents said, "Have fun and be sure to be home for dinner at 5 o' clock."

I was on my own for the WHOLE day.

Once particular Saturday, I rode my bike over to my friend Gene, who was finishing up his chores at his house.

"Hi Mr. C," I said to his dad.

"Hi, Don, you kids have fun today and be sure you are home for dinner at 5 o' clock."

"Yes sir," Gene and I said, and off we went on our own to explore our world.

First, we needed to get some supplies, so we rode our bikes and got beef jerky for the day's travel over at the little corner store with the wooden floors.

Then, with the jerky secured in our pockets, we rode over to the steepest street in our town, the dreaded Seaview Drive. Even the name was terrifying: *Seaview*. From the top of that street you could see the waters of the San Francisco Bay.

We rode, we grunted, we sweated, and sometimes we walked our bikes to the top of that incredible street.

We were relieved when we reached the top. Then, we bit off a piece of that beef jerky, looked each other in the eye, nodded, and jumped on our bikes to begin the steep descent down Seaview Drive.

It was like flying. We went so fast and raced each other. We jammed on the foot breaks and turned right and left as the wind blew furiously into our sweaty faces. A flat spot on the drive allowed us to peddle to keep the speed up, but the hill dropped off again, and we held on for dear life.

When we reached the bottom of this mountain, we laughed and laughed about our great adventure and our close encounter with death itself.

We sat down, sweaty faces beet-red with excitement.

"Well, that was fun! What time is it? Oh, it's still early! I think we can do that again and still be home for dinner," I said.

"Haha, yeah, let's go," Gene replied.

And at the bottom of that hill we started our climb up our Mount Everest.

A boy never had more fun. At dinner my parents would see a red-faced, healthy boy with a glimmer in his eye and tall tales to tell of his adventurous day.

I Remember

On my block where I grew up was the greatest time.
If you looked out your windows so many kids you would find.
Hustling and bustling adventures to take.
Every day outside a new friend you would make.
The street went up a hill, and I loved reaching the top.
Going down on a skateboard with no way to stop.
We'd even use shopping carts that would speed so fast,
And without a doubt you knew you would crash.
But that didn't matter, we were well aware
That we'd get cuts and bruises, but we didn't care.
Because as soon as that happened, we would do it again.
We'd go on and on till the day came to an end.
The sun would set and your mom would yell out your name.
"See you tomorrow and we'll play a new game."
The next day we'd be back and do it all over again.
Having fun with your friends was a reoccurring trend.
Whatever sport was in season, that sport we would play.
And if I had that football, get out of my way.
There was no stopping me, to the touchdown I rushed.
Playing on concrete sometimes we'd get crushed.
We would all laugh and say, "Did you see that hit?"
Give each other high fives, and get right back to it.
Catch us inside our home, there would be no way.
In our eyes we'd consider that a waste of a day.
I miss those days and the fun that we had,
But now I can do it with my kids and be a fun dad.

The Samurai

Once upon a time in the North East of L.A.,
There lived a young samurai who still lives there today.
You're thinking, *A samurai, really? Come on, how old?*
Trust me, my friend, she lives by the code.
Don't underestimate her skills and insult her like that.
Show her hostility and she'll definitely attack.
Those in the city knew not to doubt.
They've witnessed her skill and what she's about.
Anyone who caused malice and brought people harm
Would come across this samurai and all of her charm.
They'd think to themselves, *This will be an easy defeat.*
But before they knew it, they'd lose their hands and feet.
She didn't look for the trouble, but trouble she would find.
But within all of the chaos, she found peace of mind.
She would give them a chance to turn from their ways.
If they refused her offer, they'd end up in a daze.
She was quick with her hands and just as fast with her kicks.
Her weapon skills were amazing and you should've seen how she flips.
She moved in silence, too quick to be seen.
The ones she's defeated feel as if it was a dream.
They cannot grasp what they just faced.
They underestimated her and now they're full of disgrace.
So you better think twice before doing anything wicked today
Because you might run into the young samurai known as Nevaeh.

Moving On

Okay, my elementary comrades, today I'm gone.
I'm off to a middle school adventure; in my absence, be strong.
I know I've been a good leader as head of the class.
All the sorrow you are feeling—this, too, shall pass.
Yes, I'm the kickball champ, but I'm a person just like you.
If you stay motivated and driven, there's nothing you can't do.
If the kickball crown is what you desire,
Attack it with might, with a heart full of fire.
I might stop by on occasion to see how you're doing,
To share my middle school stories about the crowds I am wooing.
Take care of this school, it has been good to me.
But I'm not going to lie, I'm glad to be free.
I'm older now, more mature I've grown.
It's time for me to conquer a brand new throne.
Till we meet again, I bid you adieu.
I hope my foreign word doesn't confuse you.

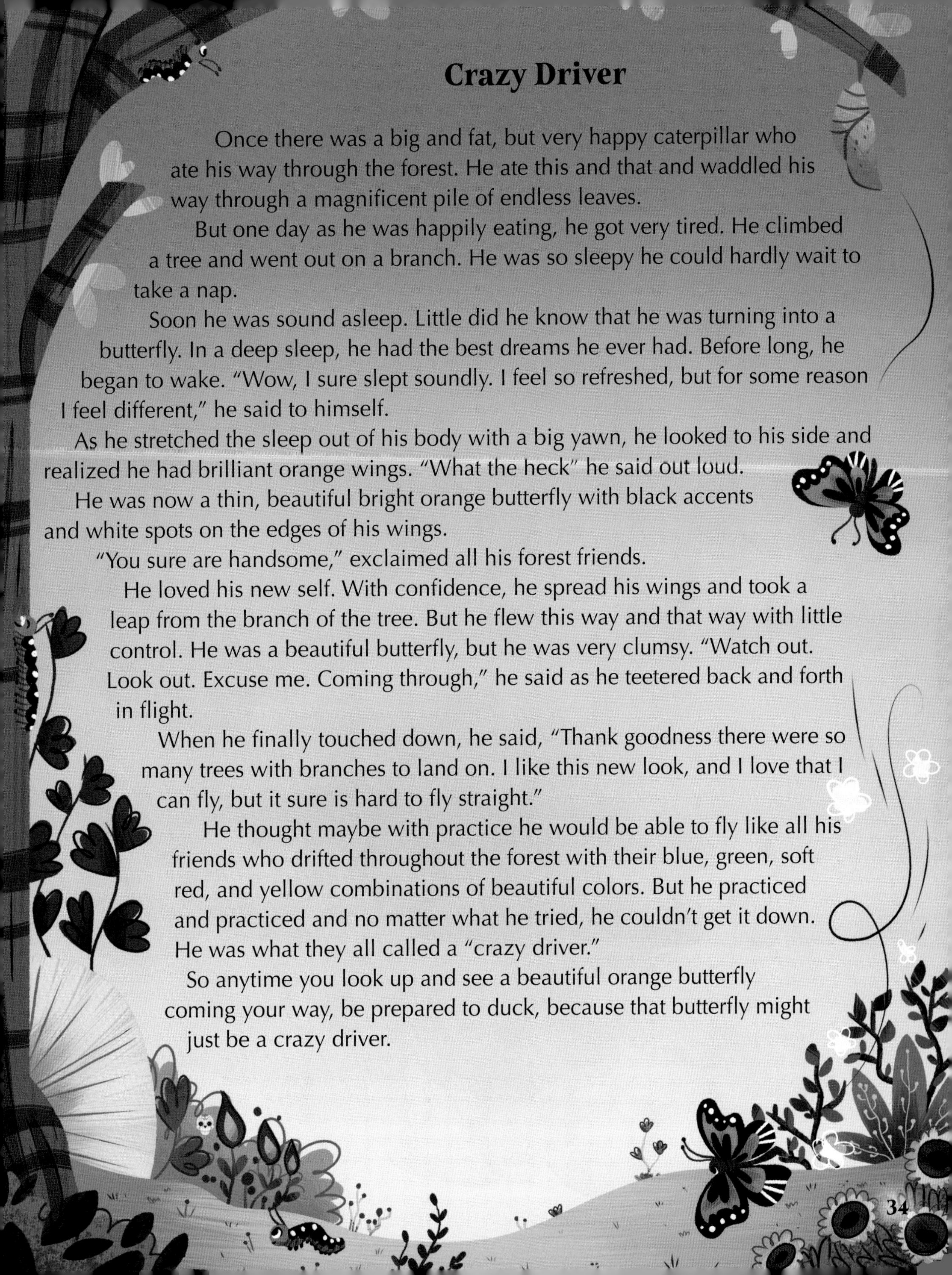

Crazy Driver

Once there was a big and fat, but very happy caterpillar who ate his way through the forest. He ate this and that and waddled his way through a magnificent pile of endless leaves.

But one day as he was happily eating, he got very tired. He climbed a tree and went out on a branch. He was so sleepy he could hardly wait to take a nap.

Soon he was sound asleep. Little did he know that he was turning into a butterfly. In a deep sleep, he had the best dreams he ever had. Before long, he began to wake. "Wow, I sure slept soundly. I feel so refreshed, but for some reason I feel different," he said to himself.

As he stretched the sleep out of his body with a big yawn, he looked to his side and realized he had brilliant orange wings. "What the heck" he said out loud.

He was now a thin, beautiful bright orange butterfly with black accents and white spots on the edges of his wings.

"You sure are handsome," exclaimed all his forest friends.

He loved his new self. With confidence, he spread his wings and took a leap from the branch of the tree. But he flew this way and that way with little control. He was a beautiful butterfly, but he was very clumsy. "Watch out. Look out. Excuse me. Coming through," he said as he teetered back and forth in flight.

When he finally touched down, he said, "Thank goodness there were so many trees with branches to land on. I like this new look, and I love that I can fly, but it sure is hard to fly straight."

He thought maybe with practice he would be able to fly like all his friends who drifted throughout the forest with their blue, green, soft red, and yellow combinations of beautiful colors. But he practiced and practiced and no matter what he tried, he couldn't get it down. He was what they all called a "crazy driver."

So anytime you look up and see a beautiful orange butterfly coming your way, be prepared to duck, because that butterfly might just be a crazy driver.

The Scorpion Queen

There was once a young girl who moved to a land
Where there was cactus, dirt, rock, and some sand.
Yet she didn't know that amongst this terrain
Something would cause her life to change.
One night while sleeping in her comfortable bed,
She stretched out her legs and kicked a scorpion's head.
The scorpion got angry and the girl it did sting,
But to the scorpion's surprise she did not scream.
So frustrated he got that he stung her once more,
Surely, he thought, she'd get up and run out the door.
What happened next, he could not comprehend,
The girl pulled back the blankets and said, "Hello, my new friend."
He thought for sure she'd panic and act all spazzy.
But she said, "Hello Mr. Scorpion, my name is Jazzy.
He thought for a moment, *This must be a dream!*
Or maybe I stung myself and now I'm seeing things.
"Are you okay, Mr. Scorpion? Have you lost your way?
Is there something I can help you with today?"
"Are you not afraid?" the scorpion asked in a trance.
The girl responded, "Of you, not a chance."
"But I just stung you," he said, "not once, but twice."
"That's okay," she said. "You still seem real nice.

"Were you cold outside, is that why you came into my bed?
My apologies, Mr. Scorpion, for kicking you in the head."
He was surprised and did not know what to say.
He felt really bad for stinging her that way.
"I'm sorry, Jazzy, for what I have done."
So he jumped off the bed and started to run.
"Wait!" she yelled. "Please come on back.
Don't keep on running, just stop where you're at.
You probably lost your home when these houses were built.
And I accept your apology, so let go of the guilt.
My room is big, there's room for two.
There's a place for me and a place for you."
"That's sweet of you, Jazzy, but I cannot stay.
I like to explore at night and sleep during the day.
Plus, you might not harm me, but someone else might."
"Will you at least consider staying some of the night?"
"Okay," said Mr. Scorpion, so back to her bed he did walk.
They stayed up the whole night so they could just talk.
"The sun is about to rise, so now I must go.
Thank you for everything and the kindness you showed.
And Jazzy, I love your room, and how it's so clean.
It was a pleasure meeting you, my Scorpion Queen."

I Love School

I don't exactly know why, but I just love school.

It could be because I like my teacher, Mr. Compton, who is fun and interesting and teaches us something new each day.

My dad makes me tell him three things that I learned each day when he picks me up from school. My teacher teaches me so much that it's easy to tell my dad three things.

Yes, I bet that is why I love school.

But...

Maybe it's the other students, all of my friends that I have at school. We play at recess, laugh, tell stories and jokes, and just have fun. We study in class, but have fun there, too. We did a science project and Elena did a study on how plants do better when you are nice to them. We all laughed and teased her, but you know what? The plants did seem to do better! We go to parties and eat pizza together; we play sports and help each other.

Yes, I bet that is why I love school.

But...

Maybe it's the theater group I belong to. We put on plays and sing together. We did a play recently *The Sound of Music*. I thought it was a strange title, but the music was wonderful and the play was a success, with all the other students and parents showing up for the performance. They were all singing along.

Yes, I bet that is why I love school.

But...

It might be the volleyball team I'm on. We are pretty good, and I happen to be pretty tall, which helps. We practice and get tired and sweaty while getting better as a team. We play games where all the other students and parents show up to cheer us on. My dad is always clapping, especially for me. My mom keeps yelling, "You go, girls!" We all laugh.

Yes, I bet that is why I love school.

Or maybe it's all of it. I do love school. My parents tell me college will teach me more, I will meet even more friends, be on sports teams, theater...I'm pretty sure I will love college.

Dear Hawaii

Dear Hawaii, it's been some time,
But every day, you're on my mind.
I miss you like crazy, without you I'm lost.
But to you I'll return, whatever the cost.
I miss your scent and that ocean breeze,
The sound of your waters and your beautiful trees.
Just going for a swim with the turtles I'd meet,
With so many fish swimming by my feet.
How about getting my board and catching some waves?
Caught up in your trance, stuck in a daze.
Walking on your beaches, on that warm sand,
Everything about you is really quite grand.
I love you, Hawaii; I mean it, I do.
And I cannot wait to come back to you.

War with the Wind

Today I declared war with the stubborn wind.
I'm making a plan to make sure that I win.
Why am I doing this, one might ask.
I'm just tired of the wind and its strong ol' blast.
Just the other day it knocked down my favorite tree
And when I play outside it will not let me be.
I went to play with my frisbee and it took it away.
Those are just some of the reasons I declared war today.
It even took my favorite cap right from my head.
Be ready, you wind, for this day you will dread.
I've got the biggest bags to set a trap
To catch the wind when I attack.
I've got a vacuum cleaner to suck that wind up.
Today is the day! Enough is enough!
I paint my face and my fatigues are on.
It's going to be a rough one—the wind is blowing strong.
So I grab my bag and attack with all my might.
Wouldn't you know it, I start to take flight!
So I release the bag and it flies up to the sky.

I can no longer see it because it flew up so high.
So I grab the vacuum and turn it on full blast,
But it starts sucking up the flowers along with the grass.
I can't believe it, the wind won again.
So I drop to the floor and think this is the end.
But as I lay there defeated, what do I see?
The frisbee I lost coming right back to me!
The wind didn't take it; on the roof is where it sat.
The wind shook it loose and brought it right back.
It doesn't make us friends; you've done other things.
But then right at that moment I hear the chimes sing.
Maybe this wind isn't so bad.
Could a misunderstanding be all that I had?
In a blink of an eye the wind is no more.
The bag that flew away lands right on the floor.
As I lay there, still battling with spite,
My dad shows up with a brand new kite.
But if there is no wind, my kite will not glide.
So I stand up and swallow my pride.
Will you forgive me, wind, for my actions that were a disgrace?
And right at that moment, I feel the wind on my face.

The Cave

Once there was a boy named Antonio who lived with his mom and dad. He had no brothers or sisters, but he wished he did.

One day he asked his mom, "Mom, can we get a horse? I would love that. I'll take care of him, feed him, and make sure he has water. Can we?"

"No," said his mom. "We don't have the room for a horse."

"But we have a big backyard," said Antonio.

"Yes," said his mom. "But the yard is not suited for a horse. It has a creek, a cave, and many trees. A horse needs a big, flat area to run and be free."

"Shoot," said Antonio, and he walked off to the backyard.

He crossed the small creek that ran through the property and walked over to the cave. It was not very big, but it was taller than Antonio. He could see the other end of it easily. So he decided to walk through it. As he walked, he wished for a horse. When he made it through the cave, he saw three beautiful horses staring at him.

What? thought the boy. *This is great.* He went to the horses and began to pet them. They were friendly and seemed to know him. He reached into his pocket and found carrots and apples, just what horses love to eat. He talked to them and walked with them.

After a while, Antonio said, "Well, I have to go home." So he walked through the cave and over the small stream to get home.

When he got home, he told his mom about the horses but she just said, "Sure, sure," and smiled at his imagination.

"Maybe we could get a big swimming pool," Antonio said at dinner that night.

His mom shook her head and said, "We just don't have room for a pool."

The next morning, Antonio was thinking about the pool as he walked through the cave to see the horses. When he got to the other side, he stopped in wonder. There was a pool there!

What fun, thought Antonio. Then he jumped right in and swam and splashed and had a very fun time. Again, after he walked

back through the cave and over the small creek, he told his mom about his wonderful day in the pool.

"Sure, sure," said his mom, smiling at her imaginative son.

Pretty soon, the boy began to think, *When I want something and walk through the cave, it is there. Maybe I have a magic cave!*

So the next time he went through the cave he thought of his grandpa who had died years ago, the grandpa who he truly loved and missed and all the fun times they had shared.

When he walked out the other side of the cave, he fully expected to see his grandpa. But no, he was not there to greet him.

Instead, there was a very large and beautiful park. Antonio walked on a path that meandered through a big lawn full of majestic trees until he came to a bench. He sat down and was thinking of his grandpa when someone said, "Excuse me, is anyone sitting with you?"

"No," said Antonio. When he looked up, he saw his grandpa smiling with pride at him. "Grandpa!" yelled Antonio, and he jumped up to hug him tightly.

They laughed, talked, hugged, and had a wonderful time together.

"You must go home now," his grandpa said. "Go see your mom and dad and enjoy your dinner."

"But," said Antonio, "I don't want to leave you."

"You'll never leave me," his grandpa said. "I'll always be with you."

Antonio gave his grandpa a great hug and then went back through the cave to return home.

"Mom, Dad, you won't believe what happened today," he said, and he told them his story with great expression and enthusiasm.

"Sure, sure," his mom said with a smile, though now she had a new thought. *What a great cave that must be. Grandpa was very special.*

I Want

I want that new bike and that new toy.
Please, oh please, I've been a good boy.
This bike is cool, but now there's one better.
My sister beats me in races, and I just cannot let her.
Speaking of new, my skateboard looks tore,
And it's out of style, let's head to the store.
Come on, please, I need what is new.
I want to be the coolest kid at my school.
Whoa! My child, keep your feet on the ground.
All this stuff you have, in it you might drown.
Don't chase the neighbors and all that they've got.
Because all that it seems, well, really it's not.
They have so many things inside of their homes.
But the parents work so much, the kids are always alone.
How about the other kids who live right down the street,
Who barely have shoes to cover their feet?
They play outside with sticks and have it quite rough,
Yet they're having a blast and don't care about stuff.
So please listen, my child, like I've said before,
Some kids might have less, and some might have more.
Enjoy what you have; who cares about new trends?
As a matter of fact, go share it with friends.
Forget about the "I wants," and enjoy the "I've gots."
Any extra stuff you have, give it to the "have-nots."
Life is always better when you share and can give.
Now that's a great life that we all should live.
There's nothing wrong with wanting something new,
It's a normal feeling we all share with you.
But we have to be careful and not take it too far.
And never let the things we have define who we are.

Oh Boy, Oh Boy

I just love taking walks. I love them every day. I walk around the neighborhood on Casanova Street. Sometimes I walk along the 12th Avenue Beach or Mission Trails, and sometimes we go to the big grass field at Quail Meadows and I run as fast as I can.

My mom, well, I think she's my mom 'cause she calls herself mom, but she doesn't look a thing like me. My dad, too, has no resemblance to me. And they walk on two legs! Haha, can you imagine? If they would only get on all fours like me, they could run a lot faster. I can always outrun them.

Sometimes they throw a ball, but I can't understand why. What's that all about?

If they throw it, they can pick it up. That's my feeling. I'm training them not to throw the ball, but it's taking them a long time to learn.

When we go on any kind of walk, I almost always have to go to the bathroom. It's a little embarrassing, but I've gotten used to them looking at me. "Good boy," they say.

And I always laugh when I go poopoo and they pick it up. What? Why? But they always do.

When we go on walks in Carmel-By-The-Sea, almost everyone we meet tells me that I'm handsome and a good boy. They talk to my mom and dad, but most of the conversation is about me. Do I run on the beach? Do I go to the grass field? And when? They want to know so we can see each other there.

People who often stop to talk to us also have kids like me. Different-looking, mostly, but smart enough to be on four legs.

Everybody in Carmel knows the kids' names but rarely the parents' names. They go by "Brandy's Dad" or "Nellie's Mom." My parents go by "Uncle Frank's Mom and Dad."

When I can, I love to hang around with all my friends: Coco, Brandy, Jessie, Nellie, Blaze, Shalom, Bo, and of course, my big buddy Gus.

Yeah, life here is pretty good for a boy like me. I hope I see you one day—just look for me, Uncle Frank! I'll probably be walking around my neighborhood with my dad and my mom.

Giana Rose Lopez

Who is Giana Rose Lopez? Well, where should I start?
How about the sweetest kid I know, who has the kindest heart?
She is always willing to help others no matter the task,
And if you're too shy to approach her, she doesn't hesitate to ask.
Did you know she's a dancer and she dances quite well?
Her movements calm the wind and tame the ocean's swell.
And boy, does she love horses, if you didn't already know.
It's like her and the horses share the same soul.
I'm serious; they come to her like they've known her forever.
Besides those two things, this girl is quite clever.
Her memory is amazing; all the facts she retains.
Sometimes I think she was born with two brains!
If I forget something, I am not worried a bit.
All I do is ask Giana because she remembers it.
Here's a little secret, but don't tell her I told:
She's an undercover ninja at only ten years old.
You can ask her if you want, but that she will deny.
It's because ninjas are secretive, but you can see it in their eyes.
She's been on many missions, fighting all kinds of foes,
Leaving death and destruction wherever she goes.
So better yet, don't ask her, please don't, my friend.
Because if you do, well, that might be your end.
That's just one side of her, just a little speck.
She's truly the girl with a big heart the last time I checked.
So if it's a friend you need who is as loyal as can be,
Well, look no further than the girl I call G!

Mars

How did I get to be the first one to stand on the planet Mars? Who knew while I was growing up that it would be me?

Yet here I stand, in the soft red powder on the surface of Mars, so many, many miles from my home in Carmel-By-The-Sea, California, United States of America, Earth.

Whoever thought I'd have to put the word "Earth" in my address? I'm the first one.

Here I stand with the American flag on my left and my spaceship, Jenny, on my right. I breathe air, but not Martian air—Earth air. My spacesuit fits me like my clothes do, the only difference is my head is in a helmet to protect me.

It is not fun to sneeze in this helmet and it is impossible to scratch my nose. Oh well!

My friends are watching me from the spaceship windows, waving and cheering me on, as the First to Stand on Mars. The stars around me are intoxicating, so bright, so full, so near.

It's like a dream that I am here. All the training, all the time learning to be an astronaut, and all the efforts of so many people got me here.

My best friend and companion for this adventure has been my dog, Uncle Frank. He walks with me, runs with me, and he was with me when I took off on this adventure. I can see him peeking out from the spaceship window.

Hey! What's he doing here?

Next thing I know, he is walking carefully down the ramp from the ship to the surface of Mars with a spacesuit on and a cute helmet around his big, red head.

"Uncle Frank! Did they make a spacesuit for you, too?" I laugh.

Uncle Frank sits next to me in the soft, red powder of Mars.

"We are going to have wonderful adventures here on Mars, and I can't wait to start."

Suddenly, I hear a strange voice that sounds like it's from a different planet. "Jamie! Jamie! Time to wake up."

"No, no, no, not yet! I just made it to Mars with Uncle Frank."

"Come on now, time for school."

"Shoot, I guess I'll have to continue our adventure tonight," I say to Uncle Frank, who wags his tail and agrees.

I can't wait for tonight.

Best Friend

I have a best friend who I love like no other.
We're as close as can be, like a sister and brother.
My best friend makes me smile when I feel really sad
And helps calm me down when I get really mad.
No matter how I feel she stays by my side
And loves to spend time with me when I go play outside.
It's like we were meant to meet and share life together.
To be honest, I couldn't have asked for anyone better.
The day shines a little brighter when she is around
And when she speaks it's a beautiful sound.
When we're together we can conquer the world—
One happy boy and one happy girl.
I'm so glad we rescued her from that pound,
Because that puppy Roxy is the greatest friend I have found!

The Red Star

Once upon a time there was a boy who loved to look at the stars at night with his dad. They would put on warm coats, bring a big soft blanket, and climb up on the roof of their house. They would lie on the soft, thick blanket, and stare at the wonderful stars. Often, Grandpa would join them when he came over.

There were so many stars, all twinkling and putting on a light show each night.

Occasionally they would see a falling star, but they went by quickly. You had to be on alert to see this very fast-moving star. We would laugh and make a wish on those stars.

"The biggest stars do not blink and twinkle, and those are planets: Mars, Venus, Jupiter and Saturn," Grandpa told us one clear night under the stars.

They were easy to spot because, sure enough just like Grandpa said, the planets didn't twinkle.

Once in a while we saw satellites go quickly and steadily across the sky. They were tiny and did not twinkle.

Once we read that the space shuttle would be flying over our house, so we waited in great anticipation, and it glided across the night sky. What fun!

Grandpa had been pretty sick, and one day, he died. I was so sad because I loved him. We had a special relationship we both enjoyed. I taught him things that were happening today that he might not know, and I kept him current, which he appreciated. He, on the other hand, told me stories about long ago when no one had a microwave oven, a computer, or a cell phone. I was always fascinated how people lived without all the things we have today.

I miss my grandpa.

One night, I was talking to my dad about how much I missed his dad while we were up on the roof on our star-watching blanket.

"I miss him too, and I know how much he loved you," my dad said.

As we looked up that night, we saw a star that we had never seen before. It was a small red star that twinkled twice as fast as the others.

My dad and I looked at the pretty star, and then each other. *I wonder if that's Grandpa, waving at us, watching us, being with us,* we both thought.

We often lie down on the roof and talk about Grandpa, the Twinkling Red Star. I feel better knowing that it is there each night.

The Best Superpower

Once upon a time, three friends were talking about what they would do if they could have one superpower.

Rosemary said, "If I could have just one superpower, I would want to fly."

"Okay, but without strength like Supergirl, what would you do?" said Sebastian.

"Well, I guess I would fly around to all my friends' houses, and my grandma's house."

"Yes, but no one could fly with you," said Sebastian.

"Mmmmm," said Rosemary. "I better rethink the superpower of flying."

Sebastian said, "I know! For my superpower, I want to be able to read peoples' minds. That would be fun."

"Not my mind," said Rosemary. "I'm always changing my mind," she laughed.

"Yes," said Sebastian. "But when the teacher gives us a test, I could read the teacher's mind to get the answers. Or other students' if the teacher was not thinking about the test."

"Yeah, I guess," said Rosemary. "But that still seems like a lot of work."

Chloe said, "I got it! I would be able to see through walls and doors for my superpower. If my mom lost her keys at home, I could look everywhere for them just by standing in one place."

"Yeah, I guess," said Sebastian. "But you could also see people in the bathroom."

"Yuck!" said Chloe. "That's not what I was thinking."

Rosemary said, "When I was on vacation with my parents this summer, we went to Italy, Austria, Switzerland, France, and Spain, and we had a hard time with all the different languages, menus at restaurants, signs to get to places, and even communicating with the people. I'm wondering if a great superpower would be to be able to talk, read, write, and communicate with anyone anywhere in the world."

"Wow," said both Chloe and Sebastian. "Being able to talk to anyone wherever you go?" They both shook their heads up and down. "That is a great superpower, maybe the best superpower ever."

All three started laughing. "You know, that is one superpower we could all have by studying different languages in school. We could get better and better at foreign languages and understand a lot of this world."

They all started to realize that they can make their own superpowers.

This Boy

They call me a boy, but I say I'm a man.
They stare at me confused, they don't understand.
I'm only twelve years old, how can this be?
What are they missing? What can't they see?
I get myself ready for school, no huff and no puff.
My mom smiles at me like that isn't enough.
I make my own breakfast and pack my own lunch,
Sometimes I even skip breakfast and just have brunch.
I make my own money by recycling cans.
I collect them all with my own two hands.
I don't need a ride to school, I just go ahead and walk.
Did I mention I wake up with my own alarm clock?
I even make sure my younger siblings get to class.
My parents tell me to do it and no questions I ask.
I just get things done, that's what I do.
If that's not a man then they have no clue.
So what if I cry when I scrape my knee?
Or if my dad helps me down from climbing high on a tree?
And I don't have a job or even pay rent.
I wouldn't mind helping, but all my money I spent.
Now that I think about it, there's more bills to pay.
And you know what, they're all due the same day!
Just being a kid, I think I should.
No need to rush it, really, I'm good.
Some say being older would be really cool.
I think I'll just worry about staying in school.
This stage in my life, it's really not bad,
I'll leave that man stuff all to my dad.

Who

We always ate dinner as a family each night and held hands to say a small blessing for the food that we had before us. We did not take it lightly that we had food on the table each night.

After the blessing we talked about how each of our days went: the good things, the bad things, and all things. This was a great time to share and get family feedback on our issues.

But one night, after the blessing for the pizza we were eating, my dad said, "I want to take tonight to ask one question about many, many things: who?"

What? What did he say? What does that even mean?

"Dad, please explain what you mean," we asked.

My dad said quietly, "I want all of us to think of who. *Who* made the flour for the pizza we are enjoying, and where did it come from? *Who* did the work to pick the plants? *Who* did the grinding of the grain? *Who* packaged the flour? *Who* took it to the market? *Who* put it on the grocery shelf? *Who* checked it out of the store so your mother could turn it into a pizza for us all to enjoy?

"*Who* grew the tomatoes for the pizza sauce? *Who* picked the tomatoes from the field? *Who* drove the truck to bring the tomatoes to market? *Who* cooked and puréed the tomatoes into a sauce? *Who* added the spices in the tomato sauce and where did they come from?

"*Who* grew the trees that became the wood that was turned into napkins so we could wipe our faces and hands off as we eat?

"*Who* brought us the water that sits in our glasses that we drink with dinner? *Who* got it all the way from the mountains to our sink?

"We often need to ask the question: who?" said Dad.

That's when we realized, we could easily keep going.

Think of the chairs we eat dinner on, the dining room table for our food, our knife, fork, and spoon – how much material did it take? How much labor? How many hours did it take and who did all this work so we don't have to use our fingers to eat our food?

Who worked on the clothes that you wear? Where did all the material come from? *Who* was responsible for all the work it took for you to be clothed?

"I want all of us to always keep the word who in our thoughts. You will appreciate your life more and you will waste less," said Dad to a quiet table.

I'll never forget that day and that meal. My dad taught me an important life lesson that night. And today I always ask, "*Who*?"

The Best Face Painter

I think I am the best face painter in the whole wide world. How do I know this? I'm in demand. My painted faces are the most realistic, most natural, and most believable. Ask anyone.

My secret?

Well, when my baby sister goes to bed at night, she likes it when I paint her face. My mom and my dad also like it when I paint their faces when they take a quick nap on the couch on a Sunday afternoon.

I make my left hand into a magical paint jar with every color in the world, and my right pointer finger becomes my paintbrush.

I carefully dip my paintbrush into my paint jar and begin my work.

For my sister, Holly, I start with chestnut brown eyebrows. I take my time with the eyebrows because they are so important, and it makes Holly giggle a bit.

Then, I paint the nose a soft color and I have to make the nose holes, so I quickly poke my finger into her nose holes. She can't stay still and laughs out loud.

Next, the lips will be a brilliant red, my favorite color. First, I paint the top lip with a gentle and soft brush, then the bottom lip with a firmer stroke of the brush. Again, she squirms and giggles. The ears I do with a swish to get the color just right, and again I have to poke my fingers quickly in her ear holes. My painting is definitely ticklish.

Now it's time to paint the rest of her face. I dip my entire paintbrush into my paint jar and gently paint her face, starting with her forehead, then her cheeks, then around her lips and her chin.

She is giggling less now and beginning to really relax.

Time for the hair. I dip all my paintbrushes into my paint jar and get just the right colors of blonde and chocolate brown.

I rub her head to get all her hair and colors just right. I do this for a long time and very lightly. Before I am done, Holly is sound asleep.

"Next," I say, and I head off to find Mom or Dad.

About the Authors

This is the second in a three-book trilogy of our stories and poems. Rocky the Rock is back with more adventures and so is Uncle Frank the dog. Many of these adventures take place in Carmel-by-the-Sea in California where Don retired with his wife, Jenny and their Labradoodle dog, Uncle Frank.

Book 2 has Don telling more of his interesting stories with good moral themes and his son-in-law Javier with more of his fascinating poems on a wide variety of subjects. Together they wrote Book 2 for all to enjoy and as a continuation of Book 1.

They are hard at work creating more stories for you to enjoy in Book 3, which is scheduled to be released in mid-2020.

Don is an Army Veteran and a graduate of the University of California, Berkeley. Don had a wonderful working career as a licensed Landscape Architect and since retiring is an Artist, Author, and currently on the Board of Directors for Papillon Center for Loss and Transition, a nonprofit helping those who have experienced the loss of a loved one.

Javier is a Marine Corps Veteran and is proud that he had the chance to serve his country. He was born and raised in North East Los Angeles (NELA) and currently resides in Northern California, in the city of Brentwood. He is happily married to his wife Holly and has four beautiful children, Antonio, Sebastian, Chloe, and Giana. Let's not forget about their awesome dog Roxy and super cool turtle Squirt, a.k.a. Mr. Turtle! Javier is currently working on his poems for Book 3. He has loved hearing about how Book 1 has put smiles on the faces of the kids who have read it, as well as their parents. He hopes Book 2 will continue to do the same. Never in his wildest dreams did he think that one day he would be able to say he is an author. He credits this new adventure in his life to his father-in-law Don Rose, who is always encouraging Javier to never give up and to pursue his dreams.